Tales II

By David Jones.

Dedicated to my mother for encouraging my imagination and always supporting me. I must also give a massive thanks to everyone who read Tales I - without you, this book wouldn't exist! I appreciate it more than you can even imagine.

David Jones (also known as storydj) has always had a keen interest in storytelling and began writing at a young age. He recently graduated from the University of Liverpool with a BA, MA and PhD in English Literature and Language. His poetry and fiction have gained a large social media following of over 1 million users across Instagram, Facebook and TikTok. Poetry books written by David have regularly ranked in best seller lists around the world. His favourite writers and influences include Gabriel García Márquez, Philip Pullman, Thomas Pynchon, Haruki Murakami and Tolstoy.

For more information on the writer or to ask questions, please reach on social media.

Do you remember me? I think we travelled together once before…
perhaps it was more than once. Perhaps it was many times. I was a
conductor on a train that carried passengers to their soulmates, until
I found my own. Now I am speaking to you from the end, but that is
alright. The end is where we all arrive at eventually.

I have learned a great many things about the worlds, and the
alternating channels of light and dark, fear and hope, love and
sorrow, that flow through everything. My life along the train tracks
taught me even more than that, though. It taught me about the
threads that bind these worlds together and offered me some small
shreds of knowledge about how they function. That is why I want to
tell you my stories. I want to understand how it all works. Is that to
much to ask? Perhaps. But I want to try.

And remember…there are many worlds, more than we can even
imagine, and we are only shades passing through.

A Story About Two Old Friends.

I heard this story from a mysterious passenger who had seen many things.

Time and Death met on a hillside one night, to discuss the nature of things.

"They think that we are friends" said Time "And that I only exist to deliver people to you, but I would give everybody more time if I could. You are my master."

"Not so" smiled Death "I spend my time waiting for you. If you stopped, there would be no reason for me to exist."

They sat in silence for some time, watching the fireflies across the meadows.

"I am so alone" said Death "Everybody runs from me."

"I am even more alone" replied Time "Because everything slips through my fingers and there's nothing that I can hold onto."

Just then, a shooting star passed through the sky, and Time and Death made the same wish at the same moment.

"I want to stop" they said.

And for just one night, Death and Time laid down their responsibilities. They threw a party in the meadows amongst the fireflies, invited the whole world to join them, and everybody was happy.

But the night went on and on, and the party grew wilder and wilder. Without Time and Death, life lost all significance. Nobody cherished anything and the world became worthless. Some wept in despair, others lost their minds until the meadows, the people and finally the whole world turned grey.

"It seems that we are required" said Death, but Time was already back at work, and Death followed.

The Rain World.

This world is one of our most frequently requested by people who want to start again. It's accessible between 1:33am and 1:37am, but only when it's raining.

The sun shines all day long in this world, and life seems normal. When night comes, it begins to rain. The rain falls until morning and it washes away the memories of everybody who lives here. When the sun rises, everybody begins again with no memories and a new life. They meet each other for the first time, experience everything all over again and make their life whatever they want it to be.

There are no regrets here because every night the rain washes regrets away too.

This world can be cruel and you will sometimes lose people who are important to you. Don't worry. I've heard that if someone is meant to be in your life, they'll be drawn to you every day.Other things can go missing too, like broken hearts and grief. Sometimes people dream of their erased memories and feel like they're living lots of different lives.

Oh, and one more thing.

Whatever you do, don't go outside when it rains. If it touches you, you will lose more than just memories. The rain destroys completely, and since everybody forgets, there won't be anyone to miss you.

Enjoy the sun :)

The Time Traveller Part I.

A peculiar man boarded the train one night, and told me this story about a Time Traveler who went too far back…

He took his time machine on an adventure to explore the past, the ancient civilisations, the first humans, the dinosaurs and then the first formative years of Earth.

Instead, he found darkness, and mist and formless figures who advanced on him with monstrous intent.

"We are the true masters of the world" they said.

Fleeing, the Time Traveller set a course for the far future, where he expected to find sprawling cities, technological marvels and intergalactic highways.

Instead, he found the same figures mocking him from the same eerie landscape.

"We are the true masters of the world" they said "We are past and future, and you only believe what we want you to believe."

Returning to his own time, the Time Traveller found the world much as it had been.

"Perhaps it was only fantasy…or a dream…" he said.

Until a voice called out to him through the darkness…

The Travelling Circus Of Lacrimosa.

Beware of The Travelling Circus. You might hear it on a windy day, just over the horizon, but you mustn't walk towards it.

Listen for too long and a ringmaster will approach. His name is Lacrimosa, and he will seem jolly and friendly. He will encourage you to visit the circus just for one night and tell you that all of your dreams will come true including fame, fortune and love.

Don't listen. This circus exists outside of time. Stay for just one night and it's already too late. You'll never be able to go home.

Everything is designed to make you forget. The candy apples will take away memories of your childhood and home. The lollipops replace those memories with memories of the circus, so you'll feel like you've always been here.

The performers feed on emotions, attention and time. The more you watch, the more of yourself you'll lose, until you have nothing left, and all you can do is watch. You'll be dragged through the darkest worlds with the circus forever.

At least that's what I've heard. Nobody knows for sure, because nobody has ever come back.

So if you see a travelling circus passing through your hometown, just look away and try to think about something else.

The Story Of How Death Was Invented.

An old passenger told me this story, but I never caught his name. Once upon a time, Death was just a child, and he didn't know who he would become.

He lived in a small cabin with a toymaker in the heart of the Black Black Forest. Carefree and happy, every day the toymaker sent him into the forest to collect wood for the toys. The toymaker carved more toys each day until his shelves were full and there wasn't room for any more. Dismayed, he inspected the toys and found that some of the older models were in poor condition. Their paint was peeling and their wood was rotting. He scooped them up, threw them onto the fire and then carved new toys to replace them.

"Look" said the toymaker "I have solved the problem of the world."

So he handed the boy his garden scythe and his long black robes.

"Now go" he commanded his little apprentice "and solve the problem of the world. That is the job I am giving you."

No matter how much the boy cried and complained, begging to stay in their little cottage in the forest, the toymaker wouldn't listen. He sent him away to solve the problem of the world. Many years later, when the toymaker was grey and old and nearly blind with age, his apprentice returned to him.

"Please..." cried the toymaker "A little more time...mercy...please."

But no matter how the toymaker begged and pleaded, his apprentice raised his scythe, sharper than anything in the world.

The Soulmate Train Part II.

Did you catch the train that takes you directly to your soulmate? Not everybody finds it, but I've heard that it appears 2:41am and 2:46am, on nights when the full moon is copper.

This train travels to the world where soulmates are created. When onboard, please remember to stay in your seat. Voices and visions from the outside will show you all of your past lives with your soulmate, but no matter how vivid the memory is, stay in your seat and stay on the train.

The conductors are the loneliest people in the world because they don't have a soulmate. If you talk about love too much, they get jealous. Hurt their feelings and they might even ask you to leave the train, and then you'll never find your soulmate again. When the train leaves the tracks, you're getting close. You might hear the stars singing. Most of their songs are harmless love songs, but some are about heartbreak and pain. The sad songs can drive you mad with sorrow, so try to hum your own tune or listen to some music.

Arriving will feel like coming home. Soulmates are born in this world, and although they might live many lives apart, they always return here. Celestial threads bind them together, from one heart to the other, and they are forever linked across every world.

Oh, but just one more thing.

Destiny doesn't always mean a happy ending, and there's no train back from this world.

The Floating City.

Would you like to mend your broken heart? I've heard that a famous doctor used to live here, but he fled to The Jungle World...

Then look out for this floating city in the sky! I've heard that it only appears to those who truly need it, so if your heart is broken, you might see it.

This city is full of magpies. They bring back stolen silver from across the worlds and store it in vast palaces in the sky. Then, the Silverheart Artisans collect it and melt it down to make silver hearts for the broken hearted.

These hearts replace your old, broken heart and your pain will vanish. The silver heart takes away any feelings of loss and love and you'll stop missing the person who broke your heart. Some people find that they can look back on happy memories without emotion.

Sometimes the silver hearts work too well. They take away all emotions, including your capacity to feel happiness, joy and peace. Some people forget everybody that they loved, and instead of family members, they see faceless figures or ghosts.

Some of the silver hearted lose all humanity. They turn into monsters, always hunting for the heart that they lost and looking for revenge. They can't enter the city because it's in the air, but they might come after you.

They often take their fury out on the magpies, so if you see a dead or injured bird, be careful.

The Weeping Forest.

Watch out for The Weeping Forest. You might see it on a rainy day, just on the edge of the horizon. No matter how tempting it seems, you mustn't go towards it.

The trees in this forest cry day and night. Once you set foot inside, the path will disappear and it won't be easy to leave. Even retracing your steps won't help.

Misery loves company, so some of the trees will tell you their problems. It might seem kind to keep them company and listen, but stay for too long and you'll never get away.

You will see colourful creatures in the undergrowth. They're friendly enough and they love to play, but spend too much time with them and they will turn hostile. I've heard that the creatures only exist to trap people in the forest.

Lots of people have become lost here, and you might see some of them weeping with the trees. Most are too sad to hurt you, but others will try to get back what they lost. Consumed by grief, they want to steal all the happiness from you. They will take your happiest memories, your joy and even your hope, so you'll be left to cry forever with the trees.

So if you see the Weeping Forest, don't walk towards it. Find someone to talk to, or give a loved one a hug.

Two Broken Hearted Friends.

Death and Love met by the roadside one night, to discuss their broken hearts.

"My heart is broken" said Death "I tear so many people from their loved ones, leave so many alone and take away people's time when they want more."

"I feel so sad" sighed Love "Because there are so many broken-hearted people in the world, and so few find true love."

Just then, a warm summer breeze swept along the road, and the stars seemed to shine a little brighter. Death and Love had an idea.

For one night, they swapped places. Death abandoned his scythe and brought love to people across the world. Love threw away her bow, picked up the scythe and brought death.

Acting as Death, Love learned that life is fragile, and even a moment of love can make it magical. She saw the profound effect of love and loss and realised the importance of cherishing every moment, no matter how fleeting.

Acting as Love, Death learned that life's limited nature makes it so valuable and special. In the end, He learned that Love is stronger than Death, and the dead live on in the hearts of those who loved them.

As the sun rose, Love and Death returned to the roadside.

"I see that love is a taste of eternity" said Love "And even you can't take it away, not really."

"I see that life is beautiful because of its impermanence" said Death "I have taught the people to value every moment."

When the sun rose, the world seemed more magical than ever before.

The Time Traveller Part II.

Did I tell you about the Time Traveller who went to the very end?

He found an old man sitting on a rock by a dried-up sea.

"Who are you?" asked the Time Traveller.

"I am the last person in the world. I sit here and wait for the end, and my heart is broken because I am so alone."

The Time Traveller looked into the sky and saw that it was empty of stars. Even the sun was pale and long dead.

"What's your name?" asked the Time Traveller.

"Some people called me Time because I have measured the universe from the very beginning to the very end. I have many names."

Just then, a dry wind whipped up over the barren sea bed. It agitated the old bones of some animal or other, which rattled and rolled along the ground.

"I don't mean that" said the Time Traveller "What's your real name? You must have been somebody once."

The old man looked up with pale, milky eyes. He stared the Time Traveller full in the face and said:

"Isn't it obvious? I am you."

The Strangest World.

This is one of the strangest worlds. It's only accessible between 2:43am and 2:54am, but once you get there time loses all meaning, so take a watch.

I've heard that your soulmate waits for you in a flower meadow in the middle of this world, but to get there you will need to pass through the Floating Mountains. Every dream you've ever had lives there, along with every nightmare.

Sticking to the paths makes navigating this world easier, but you might meet a tall figure dressed like a clown. He only speaks in rhyme, and everything he says is a lie, even the things that seem true. If you believe him even for a moment, he will find his way into your memories, replacing all the people you love, and you'll never escape.If he offers you a ticket to the circus, don't answer and walk away. If you see him again he might have taken on a different form, so be careful.

The lake in the south of this world shows you all of your happiest memories, but if you stare too hard it also shows you people you miss and even your future. Some people see familiar figures waving at them from under the water, but don't be tempted to go in. Nothing good is waiting down there.

Be extra careful when you pass through the cotton candy fields. The air smells sweet, but if you eat any of the candy you'll forget your past life, and have no reason ever to go home.

Oh, and about leaving. What makes you think this world would ever let you go?

A Warning.

I need to warn you!

Have you ever seen someone who looks exactly like you? It might seem harmless, but this is extremely dangerous.

You could see your doppelgänger in a crowd, on a train, in a busy cafe. The sight is usually fleeting and you can forget about it, but if you see a person identical to you at night, or following you, you should be careful. This is one of the worst things that can happen.

There are many worlds and many different versions of you. Some of them are happy, some are sad, and some are unrecognisable, but if one follows you, it means that they are jealous. They might be living in a bad world or their life might not be what they wanted.

Now they want to get revenge on you for living a better life. Your doppelgänger might stalk you for days, watching everything that you do. When they reveal themselves, they will try to hurt you or even kill you.

Sometimes that's enough to ease their jealousy, but it's not always the end. Some doppelgängers will take your place and try to live your life. People who were close to you might notice that something is off, so they'll be in danger too.

I've heard that it's rare for somebody to be killed and replaced by their doppelgänger, but how would anyone know?

Watch out, and if you see someone who looks identical to you, run.

Novaaris.

Novaaris is one of the strangest planets in the universe. It can be found in the constellation of Libra, orbiting the Methuselah Star.

There are many odd stories about this planet and how it affects the planets close to it.

Novaaris's seas are made of diamond and its forests are sapphire. Strange entities live amongst the sapphire. They feed on memories and light, and when they become strong enough they leave the planet to become stars elsewhere in the universe. These false stars consume the memories of any life orbiting them. Even Earth's sun might be false.

Every 891 years the diamond sea cracks open and sucks time into it, so life on the planet is wiped out, only to begin again. People live on this planet, but they aren't anything like you imagine. Years last 9071 days and on the 71st day of the 754th month everybody gathers on the opal shores and dances under the three suns.

Their songs carry across space-time, so you can sometimes hear them on a quiet night if Novaaris is in the right position. Don't listen for too long, or you might wake up in the Sapphire Forest.

The last time Novaaris passed close to Earth it caused everybody to dance until they dropped down dead. At other times it has caused wars, or everybody to dream the same dream of whales rolling through the streets. It might even cause a Love Plague, and everybody will fall in love.

So if you see a particularly bright spot in the sky, be careful.

A Dance Of Love And Death.

Many passengers have told me this story, so it must be true...

Love and Death met in a flower meadow one night, and danced to music played by Time.

At first, the dance was slow and sad. Love reflected on broken hearts, while Death thought about all those who have long since gone to the grave. Both felt sad and alone.

As the night wore on, Time changed the music that he played. The dance became quicker, like two lovers meeting for the first time. Wherever Love and Death danced, flowers sprung up, and anybody who saw them fell in love. Hearing about the spectacle, people from across the worlds visited the meadows. They watched the dance, fell in love and left to begin new lives together. When they grew old and died, their last thoughts were of the dance.

When the dance ended, Death and Love realised that they loved each other, but they could never be together.

"I must remind people of the happiness that love brings, and how precious it is because it is limited, and sometimes even fleeting" said Love

"I must remind people to tell those close to them how they feel, and to cherish every moment. Life is beautiful because it is transient, and moments are the most precious things" said Death

So Death and Love left, and only Time remained, to play his music alone.

The Astral Nexus

Did you know that worlds are always being created and destroyed? Welcome to The Astral Nexus! Please enjoy your stay, and pay close attention to any safety guidance.

Multiple universes, galaxies and realities collide here. You can experience worlds unlike anything you've ever imagined, see the origins of time and gain incredible knowledge. If you're lucky, you might even see a world being born. Some people try to enter these new worlds, but I wouldn't advise it. You can become very powerful, but also very lonely this way, and not all the new worlds are what they seem.

The capital city overlooks a point of convergence, so the people have witnessed incredible things. They are friendly enough and guests are welcome. Sometimes gigantic eyes peer out of the gaps between worlds, or a voice speaks. Even if the voice seems comforting or as though it knows you personally, don't go towards it. It might mean well, but you really don't want to hear what it has to say.

There are no dangerous entities here, but the danger comes from the world itself. Take a wrong turn and you might get lost between dimensions or even cease to exist altogether. Some people return home to find that no time has passed, or that they haven't even left yet. Others discover that centuries or even millennia have elapsed, and nothing is as it was.

Oh, and one more thing.

Be careful what you hear and see. If you witness a secret of the universe, the people will know, and you won't be able to leave this place. Some knowledge is meant to be hidden, even if that means hiding you too.

A Message From The Past.

Have you ever spoken to your past self?

I've heard that they will sometimes reach out to you, usually late at night when you're alone and there's nobody to listen.

They might reach you over the radio or you might hear their voice on a strange television channel. Sometimes they even call you.

Whatever you do, don't hang up the phone. If your past self is calling, they might be scared, or they might want to tell you something important. Sometimes the voice is just curious and wants to know what the future holds.

Most past selves want to know whether their dreams came true, whether they found true love and became the person they wanted to be. Whatever happened, try to sound happy and optimistic. Remember, they will one day be you.

Some try to contact you if they have an important decision to make. You might be tempted to change the past, but I wouldn't advise it. Changes can have unforeseen consequences and you might lose people who are important to you. You might even end up living a life that isn't your own.

Try not to tell them anything specific, because the future is supposed to be a mystery. Just enjoy the conversation, and think about how far you've come and how far you still have to go.

Who knows, you might even be able to reach out to your future self one day.

The Death Of Time.

Time fell by the roadside, so tired that he died.

At first, the people didn't notice anything different. True, the day lasted longer and the sun didn't set, but they went about their lives as normal. Some people were even pleased. Lovers could stay together for as long as they wanted, and nobody ever grew old.

With the sun forever in the sky, people threw parties that lasted for days, months and even years. All seemed well, but without Time the world began to stagnate. The days lost all value, and so did all experiences. Nothing was precious, because it could be repeated again and again. Without the prospect of love, nobody cherished anything, not even each other. People drifted apart and remained in isolation, trapped in their emptiness and misery.

Finally, Death found the fallen body of his old friend.

"Poor Time" said Death "You were so tired, and I will let you sleep."

Just then, a young child passed by on their to the nearest village. They still had hope, and were using the endless days to see every corner of the world.

"Wait" called Death after the child "I have a task for you, one to make the world happy again."

And with that, Death handed the child Time's robes, and the clocks began to tick again.

The Soulmate World.

Many passengers ask me about this world, but it isn't easy to find. Soulmates are born here. It's only accessible every 1001 years, between the hours of 2:31am and 2:33am when there's a full moon.

You should go directly to the desert, that's where soulmates are born. Their souls are made from the same particle of sand split in two, so they are always bound to each other.

Be careful in the flower meadows. The flowers sing sweet lullabies, but if you listen, you will fall asleep and wake up in a new world, with a new life and no memory of your soulmate. It might take many lifetimes to find them again.

I've heard that a giant, invisible man walks through the mountains. He will whisper all of your insecurities, fears and deepest secrets into your ear. You can sometimes catch sight of him when the sun is at the right angle, just don't stare too hard.

Whenever soulmates are born in this world, a new star appears. You'll be able to see that star wherever you end up and whichever life you live. You'll feel a connection when you see it, so you'll know that it's yours.

Oh, and just one more thing.

This world often appears in dreams. You will be with your soulmate, so you might wake up heartbroken. Don't worry, eternity is on your side so you'll find them eventually.

The Burning World.

You wanted to know about the world where bad memories are destroyed?

The fires in the Burning World burn painful, sad and traumatic memories first, but if you stay close to them for too long, they'll start to burn good ones as well. Stand near a fire for long enough and you'll lose everything: childhood, family, friends and who you were.

People in this world live by the sea and only venture inland when their hearts are broken, or they have lost somebody who they can't live without. Huge infernos burn there, where cities used to stand and thousands of people lost their memories. You might see them, wandering lost across the ash fields. I wouldn't recommend speaking to them. Frightened people can do terrible things.

Travelling inland is difficult, but if you get far enough you'll find the site of the first fire. This is the biggest inferno, and the flames are powerful enough to burn what's to come. Not many people return from there, and if they do, they find that they have no future.

Watch out for lava flows in this world. They travel towards the sea, carrying the memories of everybody from inland. When the lava hits the water it cools, and releases those memories into the air. Bad memories make foul, toxic vapour, and if you breathe it in, you might inherit somebody else's pain.

Breathing in good memories can be pleasant, but it isn't healthy to try to live somebody else's life for too long.

A Message We Sometimes Hear On The Train.

"Oh, I'm sorry. Did you think you were dead? I get that a lot...

Not everybody is taken at the right time. If that happens to you, then you might come back. You will be feeling confused, but most of the recently returned try to go back to the people they love.

I wouldn't advise it. Your loved ones might not react how you expect. Instead, wait for the Limbo Train. You shouldn't have to look too hard: it will find you, usually at night in places that you feel happiest.

This train only appears to the recently returned. It will take you on a journey across all the worlds, but also through time. You will see your past, all of your happiest moments, and even some of your past lives. If you're lucky, you might even see visions of the people you loved. Keep the blinds closed when you pass through the desert. There are mirages here, and they will show you all of your future lives. This is knowledge that nobody should have, and it has driven some of the passengers insane.

This train is forever on the tracks, but it does make stops. Don't worry, the conductors will let you know when it's time to get off. Death will be waiting on the platform, but there's no need to hurry. Take as long as you want. The conductors are patient.

And please remember...

Whatever you do, don't try to get off before your stop. You will end up in the space between life and death, left to roam forever without form, hope or love."

The Clockwork Dominion.

Did I tell you about the world where time is completely under humanity's control?

Adjusting a clock in The Clockwork Dominion adjusts the flow of time. There are vast clockwork cities in this world, as well as clockwork towns and smaller, clockwork villages. Time moves differently in each place, so staying in touch with far-away friends is sometimes difficult. Too many adjustments or contradictory changes can cause chaos, so the clocks are controlled by the Time Keepers. They decide how long a day should last, how quickly time should pass, and whether any adjustments should be made to go forwards or backwards.

Only the rich, the powerful and the influential can become Time Keepers, so most people don't get a say in how time flows. Every so often, two Time Keepers with conflicting interests disagree about time, and a war breaks out. Time goes haywire and the world loses all sense of itself. If the war is particularly bad, you might even feel temporal changes in your world. During these wars, the Time Keepers are usually safe, and it's the everyday people who suffer. When the fighting stops, time returns to its usual flow and the people talk about destroying the clocks altogether and letting time behave naturally.

The Time Keepers don't want to lose control of their world, though, so this will never happen. Life returns to the way it was with many promises of peace, until the next war.

The Clockwork Dominion is open to visitors, but please take a watch. Lose track of time here and you might never leave.

The Memoraculus

Is there a memory you would like to relive? Then look out for The Memoraculus! Lots of passengers ask about him, so let me help.

You will only find him in the world between sleeping and waking when reality and dreams blur, and memories seem real.

He collects memories and stores them in snow globes. The most beautiful memories make the most beautiful globes. Give the globe a shake and you'll see your memory. Smash the globe and the memory will be set free, so you'll be able to relive it. Just make sure that The Memoraculus is nearby so that he can catch it again or it will be lost forever.

You can experience a memory as many times as you like, so long as you can afford it. The Memoraculus takes payment in time, so the more memories you relive, the less you will eventually make. Some people have lost their futures this way.

Oh, and just one more thing.

Bad memories can be identified as dark clouds inside the globes. If you pay The Memoraculus enough, he will destroy a bad memory for you by smashing the bottle.

Be careful.

Destroying a memory also destroys all the lessons associated with it, and you might even end up forgetting people you loved.

Wake Up!

Dreams are significant, and many people fall asleep on the train, even me. Once, I heard this voice speaking to me in my dream.

"Wake up…wake up…wake up. You can't stay here forever!

Everything in here exists to pull you deeper into the dream. If you see any of these things…please…this isn't real life. Try to wake up.

Tall faceless figures in empty car parks or shopping malls. They'll wish you a happy birthday, offer you cake and invite you to your party…but please don't go with them.

A field full of houses that appears suddenly. Just keep walking and don't knock on any of the doors. If you do, The Singing Lady will invite you in, and you don't want that.

Staying awake shouldn't be difficult because you're already asleep, just don't eat any fruit. It will send you to sleep and make you dream. One dream naturally leaves to another, and if you get trapped inside a dream within a dream within a dream, you'll never wake up.

You won't see your reflection here, apart from in a swimming pool that appears in places it shouldn't be. The reflection might even speak but the water has massive gravity, the pool is bottomless and it will pull you into the deepest parts of the dream.

What's that? You prefer the dream to real life? In that case -"

Two Entities.

Once upon a time, there was only one world and two entities.

Light and Dark lived together in their world, but they weren't always friends. Light was full of energy and loved to create. Dark loved silence and stillness, and understood that things must be destroyed for them to begin again.

Eventually, the two couldn't live together anymore. At first, they tried to divide their world into two, but the border of Light's domain crossed into Dark's, and vice versa. Finally, the two went to war and fought each other in a long and cataclysmic struggle.

Their fighting tore the world apart, blasting it open at the seams and creating huge cracks. Light and dark seeped through these cracks, creating more and more worlds in a sudden flurry. Some were destroyed over the course of the war, but many more were created where there had once been nothing.

Neither Light nor Dark could defeat the other, and they realised that their powers were roughly equal. They would have to coexist, and there would have to be peace. Exhausting their war, Light and Dark met as friends to look over what they had made.

"We have done all of this" said Light "So now we will have to look after it."

"Things will be better if we do that together" replied Dark "We will need things like Time, Love, and Death."

So the two of them went to work.

The Gaps Between Worlds.

Wherever there are worlds, there are gaps between worlds. A gap between worlds is oblivion, a place where even reality cannot reach. Nothing exists there, and if you fall into a gap, you won't exist either.

Gaps aren't always easy to spot. You might wander into one without noticing because it will initially resemble the world you came from. Shades of everybody you know will be there, and you might be able to live your life normally. Some people have gone on like this for years without noticing anything different.

The longer you stay, the further you travel from the real world. People will look at you with empty eyes. Familiar places will seem a little strange. Stars will fade one by one from the night sky before disappearing altogether.

After that, the darkness comes. It takes everything piece by piece, including you, your thoughts, memories and everything that you were. Oblivion is the natural state of a gap between worlds, and once the darkness comes it will never go. There will be no more life, no more lights, and no more world. Some people say that this is the ultimate fate of everything, but I'm not sure.

There's no need to panic or struggle!

You were doomed the moment you stepped in, so you don't need to waste time and energy trying to escape :)

The Janitors.

Did you stop believing in the worlds? Just for a moment? Push those thoughts to the back of your mind, or you could be in danger.

I'm not sure who made the janitors, whether they made themselves or whether they've always been here, but they can appear in any world. They inhabit empty shopping malls, offices, schools after hours and anywhere else that needs to be cleaned. If you see them, they might look harmless, but they perform an important function.

The janitors clean doubts from the worlds and maintain reality. If you doubt your world even for a moment or question its reality, a janitor will know. Even doubting the existence of the other worlds or the multiverse is enough to summon a janitor. They might not come straight away, but the more you doubt and wonder about reality, the more certain it is that they will find you. The janitors travel in groups, and most of the time they will wait until you enter an empty space. Even an empty house will do.

By the time you see them, it's much too late. If you're lucky they will put you to sleep and you will dream your life away, but not many people are lucky. The janitors will sweep you out of reality altogether, so there's nothing left of you to doubt.

They can't be stopped or fought, and running away won't help. Once you're gone, it will be as though you never existed, and nobody will remember that you ever were. Some people say that the janitors are just a legend, but I believe in them with all my heart.

So just believe in it all, please? In your world, in the other worlds, in reality. Believe in it. Believe, believe, believe…

The Magistratos.

Have you ever wondered where your wishes go? Don't worry. They aren't lost, and they might even come true.

Every wish you make is sent directly to the Magistratos who live in the Citadel Of Wishes. Every wish is recorded automatically by a huge printing press and then stored in an underground library for sorting. Some will come true one day, but because there are so many wishes and it takes so long to sort them, it might not be in your lifetime.

The Magistratos file every wish according to its world of origin and owner. Some of the files are vast, but some people don't make any wishes at all. Next, wishes are sent to the Examination Chamber where each is studied on its merit. Some wishes are impossible to grant, others aren't feasible and some might even be dangerous. These need to be destroyed. After that, the wish passes through lots of different chambers and rooms where it is studied, categorised and its effects weighed. If the Magistratos approve, then the wish is sent to the Sala Exauditionis.

This is the final room where wishes are granted. If you're lucky enough to have a wish get here, then your life is about to change.

Oh, but please remember.

There are many worlds, many people and even more wishes. The Magistratos sort wishes in the order that they arrive, so some are only granted when it's much too late. Don't lose heart. Someone is listening, and someone wants your wish to come true, no matter how long it takes.

The Memory Hospital.

Is there a memory you would like to forget? Then this world is for you!

Open your bedroom window between 4:41am and 4:53am. If you hear the sound of distant sirens, you'll know that you've found it.

The hospital is in an old rose garden, but be careful on the way. The gardeners stayed here for too long, so they have no memories or feelings left. They will ask you to look at the flowers but don't listen. They want to harvest your feelings to replace their own.

This hospital exists between worlds, so expect to meet lots of patients. Some of them are friendly enough, but others have a lot to forget. They might even want to take some of your happiest memories for themselves.

The queue in the waiting room is long, but when it's your turn, the doctors will ask what you would like to forget. Heartbreak, grief, sorrow, missing someone, unrequited love…these can all be taken away with a simple procedure!

If you're very lucky, you might even lose the capacity to hurt.

Please don't go downstairs. This is an experimental ward where the doctors will offer to give you new memories. These can be as happy as you like. Be careful. The doctors will tempt you with all kinds of memories, but if you add too many, you will lose who you were.

And remember…big smiles all round :)

The World Of Unending Autumn.

This world is only accessible on the final day of Spring. Open your front door between the hours of 11:23pm and 12:01am. If you can smell wood smoke, you'll know that you've found it.

It's Autumn every day in this world and the trees are always golden. There's no shortage of sweet, ripe fruit to eat and plenty of autumn festivals in the towns. Fireworks, lanterns, dancing and celebrations happen everywhere in this world. Make a wish on the gigantic, copper coloured Harvest Moon and it might even come true.

Just don't venture too far into the woods. Autumn is the season of decay, and here that decay is unending. Fallen leaves, rotting vegetation and spoiled fruit pile up in the forests. The people try to clear it away, but only on the outskirts. All the decay releases vapours that congregate in deep woodland and take the form of wraiths.

Trapped in the unending Autumn, they drift between the trees searching for victims. Anything they touch immediately starts to decay, including humans. I've heard that there are huge populations of these wraiths hidden in the forests and that one day they will spill into the towns. If that happens, everything will fall into ruin.

So enjoy this world while you can, and remember to light a lantern every time the moon rises.

Oh, and I was supposed to tell you.

Autumn is the season when the veil between life and death is at its thinnest. Don't be alarmed if you see some people who have died or other strange sights. These are just passing through from the World of the Dead. You might even recognise some of them, but it's best to let them go on their way.

Why Is My World So Empty?

This message reached us one day, over the radio. We tried to trace it without success. I don't understand it, and I can't imagine where this world could be, but the person sounded afraid.

"Are you wondering why my world is empty? I think I made the wrong wish at the wrong time, or I didn't wake up from a dream.

The streets are empty. The shops too, and the hospitals. The movie theatre plays films about my life on a constant loop. Sometimes I sit there for hours, reminiscing and trying to work out whether any of it is real.

The TV plays out the start of a warning, but the message ends before it says what it's about. The radio is the same. Everybody I loved is gone, but when I visit the graveyard, all the tombstones are blank, as if nobody ever was.

Sometimes at night, I hear music from a fairground or circus, but no matter how I try to follow it, I never find the source. I don't know whether it's real or a dream.

Yesterday a train stopped at the station close to my house. I know because a ticket arrived in my letterbox. Who posted it? I doubt I will ever know, but the train is meant for me.

It will take me far away, but I haven't given up on this world just yet. I'll stay for a little time. Please think of me, and remember me. My world will seem less empty, then."

False Stars.

Bad things can happen if you wish on the wrong star.

These entities are born in sapphire forests on a distant planet, on the very edgy of the known universe. They feed on memories and light, and then when they get strong enough they leave the planet altogether to become false suns somewhere else in the universe.

Planets and whole galaxies orbit these false suns. Even your own sun might be false. You would never know. The stars feast on the memories of every living creature orbiting them. At first, they only take small, distant memories, but the longer you live, the bigger and more important memories they'll steal.

If you feel like you've forgotten something or someone important, no matter how small the detail, you might be orbiting a false star.

Wishing on these stars is even worse. A wish forms a connection between you and the false star, even if it's far away. It won't just take memories. It will steal hopes, dreams and everything that you desire. If your wish doesn't come true or the opposite happens, you might have wished on a false star.

If your dreams never come true, then you certainly have. Sometimes, it's better to keep your hopes and desires to yourself.

The Mountain World.

Is there something you would like to know? Then the Mountain World might be the world for you!

The higher you climb in this world, the thinner the air gets. It makes thinking easier, and the wind tells secrets about the world. The people at the top of the mountains gain incredible knowledge. Some develop futuristic civilisations, others work to advance the sciences and make stunning discoveries.

Others stay in the valleys, away from the thin air and the whispering wind. These lowland areas might not be advanced, but the people are happy. They go about their lives searching for things like love and happiness, rather than knowledge.

A giant mountain in the centre of this world climbs well above the clouds. I've heard that the ultimate knowledge lives up there, and anybody who can make the climb finds it. The people are afraid of the mountain because nobody ever comes back, so the knowledge is either too wonderful or too terrible to return from.

People who visit this world usually head directly to the highest peaks, but I wouldn't recommend it. You might end up returning home knowing too much, and with great knowledge comes great loneliness. Some people left this world only to find that they were shunned back home, or that people were jealous.

Oh, and remember. The people in this world have learned not to question the source of the knowledge, or who is behind the whispering wind. We can learn a lot, but some things are better off unknown.

An Overheard Conversation One Morning.

"I met a stranger by the river, who told me that the world had ended, but only on the other side of the river.

"Look across" he said "It's all over for them! But we're alright."

I squinted across the river. Everything looked normal, but there were no signs of life.

"What happened to them?" I asked.

"Who cares? It's alright here."

We sat side by side in the sun, and after a while, the stranger pulled out a fishing rod. The rest of the afternoon passed in sunny peace. We fished and talked, laughed and joked, and forgot all about the end of the world on the other side of the river.

When evening came and the river turned ember, the stranger told me:

"Come back tomorrow. I will still be here."

So I visited him the next day. We fished again, and this time the stranger brought a picnic for us to share. Some rubble floated along the river, and dark shadows massed on the other side, but we paid them no attention.

When evening slipped over the world and the river turned dark, the stranger told me:

"Come back tomorrow. I will still be here."

I returned the next day, and as promised, the stranger was still sitting by the river. It flowed differently now, swollen and angry and full of debris. A chill hung in the air and peculiar noises emanated from the opposite bank.

"It's nothing" smiled the stranger, drinking wine with a grin on his face "We're fine over here."

We ate and drank and even played music, and at the end of the day, when the moon hung low like a rotten apple, the stranger said:

"Come back tomorrow. I will still be here."

Except the next day, he wasn't there. Darkness spilt across the river in an unstoppable flow, corrupting and destroying the forest, the fields, the plants and the birds. I turned to flee, but the darkness was behind me, too, and on every side. My world was ending at last, and me with it."

The Somniorum.

Go to a bench overlooking any city at 3:59am. If you see a lone figure sitting there, watching the city lights, don't be afraid. Sit down and talk to them. They'll love the company.

This is the Somniorum, and he is the last of his kind. When it's time for the day to end, the Somniorum snuffs out the sun and pulls the moon into the sky. When the night is over, he douses the moon and raises the sun again.

Once, that was all that he did, but over time the Somniorum learned to take on other duties. He saw how sad people were, and how the sadness from their day would give them bad dreams at night. He saw how even happy people can have bad dreams too, for no reason. Desperate to help, the Somniorum stole people's nightmares and dreamed them himself. If you remember the start of a bad dream, but then a feeling of happiness and contentment, he's probably visited you.

Over time, the nightmares transformed him into something monstrous, so he always keeps his face hidden. People are terrified of him and run away whenever they see him, but he only wants to help the world. His is a lonely existence, so please sit with him for a while.

Oh, but there is one thing you should remember. The Somniorum is looking for somebody to take over his role so that he can retire and find peace at long last. You might want to help him, and the job might even seem tempting, but be careful. If you try to take the darkness away from too many people, you'll have no light left for yourself.

The Forgetful Train.

This train only appears to those who have lost someone or need to forget a person. I don't know exactly how to find it, but I've heard that it seeks out people who need it and carries passengers to a new world where there is only peace.

When onboard, pay close attention to everything that you see. You will pass through a world where rivers of tears flow upwards and mountains float, a world where gigantic entities play sad songs day and night, and many others.

If you try to ignore them or close the blinds, they'll just appear again and then the journey will go on forever.

If a smartly dressed man with a moustache sits close to you, get up and change carriage. He will offer to bring back the person you lost but trust me, you don't want to accept his deal. The conductors are heartbroken, not because they lost someone, but because they have nobody to miss. Talk to them as much as you want, just don't mention love.

The journey is long, but I've heard that it's different for each passenger. Don't get off before your stop or you'll get trapped in the wrong world and never find the train again.

And please remember....

Peace doesn't always mean forgetting, and some memories are forever.

The World Of Unspoken Words.

Is there something you wish you had said? Someone you wish you could speak to, or unspoken words trapped inside?

Then this world is for you! All unspoken words go here, where they're stored in a gigantic switchboard. The operators work day and night to send the words where they're supposed to go, so if somebody left your life before you had a chance to tell them what was in your heart, don't worry. The operators are working on it right now.

They send messages across all of the worlds, between soulmates separated in different universes, lovers who haven't met yet and even people who aren't alive any more. There are lots of lines so it can take some time for a message to get through, but it will always get there in the end.

Messages are delivered through dreams and might even arrive as strange symbols that you'll need to decipher. You might suddenly remember someone who you thought you had forgotten, recall an old song or even find a photograph. This means that the operators are trying to get a message through to you.

If a message can't be delivered straight away, it's stored in a vast underground library. You can visit and wander through the aisles of unspoken words. They tell a history of love, heartbreak, sorrow and hope, but don't touch them. Words are meant to be spoken, so leave them be until their time comes.

And if you sense something significant in the world around you, pay close attention. You never know what it means or who sent it.

The Triplets.

The Triplets are three planets orbiting a black hole on the very edge of the known universe, close to Galaxy Candidate HD1.

Time is weird on these planets because they are so near to the Event Horizon of the Black Hole. This means that they simultaneously have and haven't been destroyed.

On Thalia, time moves much slower. People can easily revisit their memories because they are still happening. Days last for centuries and loss is uncommon because people don't age or die. The poles of this planet lean towards the black hole, so there are inescapable time loops.

On Aglaia, time moves much quicker so the planet is technologically advanced. Inhabitants can have anything and everything that they want and bad times are quickly over. Civilisations come and go in the blink of an eye, and so do lives. Time moves so quickly at the equator that people can see themselves arriving.

Be careful of Euphrosyne. All of time is happening at once there, from the very beginning to the very end of the universe. This planet is feared by the occupants of Thalia and Aglaia because its orbit affects their time, making it jump around erratically. It also shows them their futures.

Catching a glimpse of Euphrosyne even through a telescope will alter how time behaves around you. You might lose or gain days, and the passage of time can speed up or slow down, so you won't be on the same timeline as the world around you. Returning to normal life won't be easy, and the people close to your might sense that something is wrong.

If you're really unlucky, you might even see yourself staring back.

Navigating The Station Between Worlds.

You were searching for The Station Between Worlds? Let me help you...

Trains from this Station travel to all of the worlds, and the conductors are friendly. If you aren't sure of your stop, they will always be there to remind you when it's time to go. Lots of people ask me where to find the Station, but it depends on where you are coming from. Some worlds have lines leading directly to it, in others, you might have to look for secret gateways in strange locations, or even make a wish. Sometimes the Station is only accessible in dreams, but that doesn't make it any less real.

When you arrive, you should head directly to the departures board. The board is vast, so it's useful to have a good idea of where you want to go first. You will see a long list of worlds and platforms. Be careful. Some people have been known to stand at the board for days and even longer, hypnotised by all the worlds and locations.

Get your ticket from one of the ticket desks. You'll find a desk on every floor, so choose one that's close to your platform. The Station spans countless levels. Some people even say that it's infinite, and that might be true. I certainly haven't seen all of it, and I know that I won't now. Elevators fly between the floors and platforms in the blink of an eye, so you won't have to walk far. When you reach your platform, it's just a matter of waiting, but you might have to wait for a long time. Some of the worlds are far away, and it takes a long time for the trains to return.

It's not unknown for a passenger to wait most of their life to make a single trip.

You Have Been Dreaming For Too Long.

Do you remember the voice that spoke to me in my dream? I remember it vividly, even now. I have come to realise that there is another reality, no less real than this one, that is only accessible in dreams.

The voice spoke to me again recently…

"Oops!! You have been dreaming for too long. Now you can't wake up. Please choose your new reality.

The Office.

You won't be alone in The Office! Workers sit at their desks for all of eternity. I don't know what they're doing, but they won't respond if you speak. If you find an empty desk you can sit and do some work yourself, but the tasks are never ending and you won't get anything for completing them. If you see the Office Manager, run. They want to trap you at a desk forever.

The Field of Houses.

It's safe here, so choose a house. This field is infinite, so you probably won't have any neighbours, but that's for the best. If someone knocks on your door, hide. It might be the Singing Lady, and you don't want to speak to her.

The Library.

The books here contain all the secrets of the universe, but a lot of them are gibberish and it might take a long time to find what you want. You probably won't run into The Librarian, but if you do, hide. She traps people in books, and then you'll just be another sad story.

The Mall.

Enjoy the abandoned arcade, the endless stores and relax by the fountain. Rumour has it that there's a travel agent somewhere in here who will sell you tickets to escape the dream, but I've never heard of anyone who found it, and the price would be high.

The Carpark.

You will find many empty cars here! Who did they belong to? Better not to ask questions. You can get in any car, but the roads are blocked and even if you do manage to escape, you will just go deeper into the dream. A parking attendant appears after dark, so don't let them find you in a car."

The Conductor's Story Part 2.

And now I would like to tell you my story, or at least…the end of it.

It didn't even hurt, or at least I couldn't remember the pain. All that remained was the aching sensation of loss, of her hand reaching, of mine reaching back…and then a gigantic blank. Something must have stopped us from touching, but the loss was so absolute that I knew I would never be able to grasp the memory. A beach stretched out ahead and behind me, apparently forever. Waves rolled and broke along the tideline, eddying back and forth in the sand. The sun gleamed directly overhead.

"I have lost someone important to me" I said into the silence "But I can't remember exactly who."

All that remained was the shape and complexion of the loss, with nothing specific to attach it to. I must have opened my eyes at some point and found myself here, but it already seemed as though I had been sitting on the beach for as long as I could remember. All memories of what went before were gone. Only the emotions remained. I possessed some vague sensations of a lost "home," of vanished "family" and "friends," but these were only feelings with no substance behind them. All that I had left was the sand, and the sound of the sea slipping towards me like a daydream.

Squinting into the sun I wondered whether I caught sight of something on the very precipice of the horizon, something bright and pure and unfathomable, but the vision was gone as soon as it appeared. The sea stretched on and on until it disintegrated into a haze. Welcome to the Final World. There are many names for it, and I never believed that it existed. To test my physicality, I scooped up a handful of sand and let it fall through my fingers. I was intact and seemed much as I had been, complete with a broken heart. I had lost her, of course, in the final moments. Now we would never find each other again.

My previous life consisted of trains, that much was certain. I still maintained a sense of them and the endless tracks winding through the endless worlds. My passage was restless until I met her, but… we were not side by side for long. Would my next life consist of trains too? Would the winding tracks of the worlds carry me back to a similar type of life, or would I be a different person in a different place? Why sit and wonder? There was nothing to suggest that I would be forced to leave this place and even less that I would encounter anybody else. I clambered to my feet and started walking.

Nothing changed. The beach proceeded without dune or hollow, undulation or inlet. The sea neither advanced nor receded and the waves always broke at the same point, washing a little stream of foam up the shore and disturbing the sand. I wandered down to the shore and squinted out, trying to catch sight of that light across the water, but this time nothing distinguished itself. Struck with an urge to throw something into the sea, I searched around the tideline for a rock or a pebble but found nothing. Sand, water, sun and sky. Nothing else. No rocks no plants no people no distance no time.

I stooped, tried to write my name in the tideline but realised that I had forgotten it. Instead, I scraped out the rough shape of a train and then watched as the tide wiped it clean.

"Well then" I said to myself and continued to walk because there was nothing else to do.

With no way to gauge distance on that endless beach, I decided to try and set up a system of waypoints that would at least help me to determine scale. Forming handfuls of sand into a mound I walked and walked until the mound shrunk, until it sat on the brink of the horizon. A few more steps and it was out of sight. I tried to retrace my path, but no matter how long I walked, I couldn't find my mound of sand again. Even this tiny loss made my heart ache, and I mourned the loss of the mound - so harmless - for many steps.

I wondered whether it would be possible to sleep in such a place and whether my body (if my form remained physical) required sleep. The sun had not moved an inch in the sky, so there would be no night and the light would almost certainly keep me awake. I lay down on the warm sand, shut my eyes, fell asleep almost instantly, dreamed of nothing and then woke up again.

All of time might have passed, or no time at all, but my thoughts were a little clearer. I picked up a handful of sand and let it fall through my hand, every single grain, and then to make sure that I wasn't holding onto any more I washed my hands in the sea. The water was tepid - neither warm nor cold - but the tide exerted a gentle pressure as it receded, as though the water was returning to a point of distant singularity far across the horizon.

"Every grain of sand…" I said to myself and nearly laughed aloud at the foolishness and hubris of humanity.

It is a well-known fact that all the worlds are yet to be discovered and that there are many which are beyond even our wildest imagination. Despite this logical and mathematical fact, the Station Between Worlds has always maintained the absurd aim of making every world reachable by train and incorporating them all into the network. If every grain of sand on the beach represents a world, then the minuscule fraction of worlds discovered and made reachable is so small as to be statistically irrelevant. They will never do it, are making themselves look like madmen for even talking about it. For a moment I thought that I had better tell one of the managers, but quickly realised that the Station Between Worlds was no longer my concern.

"What fools we all are" I said to myself, not sadly "And how small."

There must be worlds that have never even heard of the Station, never seen a train and never will. If I were to live another life, perhaps I would end up somewhere where there are no trains and no journeys. Perhaps it might be a quiet life in the countryside, in a small cottage. I would only leave to visit the village, where nobody even dreams of the wider world, least of all multiple worlds.

The idea of another life reminded me of my mysterious loss and I began to walk again, struck with a heartache that rolled through my thoughts like the waves. I traced a path closer to the sea this time, letting the tide wash over my feet. When I looked back, I saw no footprints and no trace that I ever was. To live another life necessarily meant the utter erasure of my previous one. With it would fade the sensation of loss, but I wanted to cling to that. To let go of it would be to let go of hope.

Thus passed the time, if time even existed in that place. I made my way along the endless beach beneath the unshifting sun, sometimes strolling, sometimes running, sometimes hardly moving at all. Of course, I knew about the stories and the legend of what to do next. Pick up a handful of sand and let it fall through your fingers. When only one grain remains, close your eyes and hold tight. You will open them to a new world and a new life, with no memory of the beach.

I could have crouched down and picked up the sand at any moment. Nothing stopped me other than a vague sense that I wasn't ready yet. Sometimes I would sit for hours, staring out to sea and trying to recall who I had been. Peace washed over me, a peace more profound than I had ever experienced before. Who would leave such a place for a new life? A life that would doubtless contain moments of joy and happiness, but also of profound sorrow, of pain…and there I was on the beach with nothing to worry about, nothing even to think about until -

One day a blot appeared across the sand, on the edge of the horizon. At first, I wondered whether it was just my imagination conjuring shapes to fill the emptiness, but the dark spot moved and was coming towards me. It took the form of a person. Accustomed to emptiness, my first reaction was shock mingled with inexplicable fear. I wondered whether I ought to turn back along the beach and then keep running so that the figure would never catch me up.

Instead, I made my way down to the sea and looked out again, searching the furthest reaches for some trace of the light I had seen upon my arrival. Nothing. Only water. Only sand. And that distant figure drawing ever closer. They were in no hurry, and my fears began to diminish. I found a stone at last and skimmed it across the waves. One skip, two skips, three…four and then it sank into the depths. The figure drew closer, had obviously seen me, was heading directly for me…

And then all of a sudden the sun caught her at a peculiar angle, and she was familiar. I knew her. I had always known her. Everything else was gone. All the places, the trains, the worlds, the people and memories, were long vanished and would not be retrieved. Only her face remained. She approached as though she had something urgent to say, but when she reached me she stared in silence. The sea lapped against the shore, waves rolling and breaking, shifting all the worlds, ending some, creating new…on and on…always and forever…

"Hello?" she said at last, looking bewildered "I have lost someone important to me…but I think I remember who."

END.

Oh…but there is one more world that I would like to tell you about. Ever since I told you my story the first time, more and more people have come to me with tales about this place.

It is both like and unlike the others. I don't think I have visited, but I think you might have. You might even be there now. If you are, please enjoy it. Savour every moment, and this can be your favourite world…

The "Real" World.

There is a world that some people call the "real world." I think they believe it's the only one, but I'm not sure.

Lots of things are possible in this world and many people have dreams. Dreams can make life beautiful. Children cherish them but a lot of adults let them go.

Be careful. Stay away from your dreams for too long and you might forget about them altogether, and be left empty. Death comes to this world often, and He doesn't distinguish between those who followed their dreams and didn't. People who give up on their dreams turn into faceless entities. Not outwardly, but in another way.

This world has something called Love, and lots of people look for it. Not everybody finds it and not all stories have happy endings, but even knowing love for a short time makes life in this world beautiful.

There are vast cities here, oceans, a frozen North and South and deserts in the middle. I've heard that people sometimes feel their lives are meaningless, but I think you make your own meaning.

Some say that there is no magic in this world, just because it isn't easily visible. I don't agree. I think this world is as magical as people choose to make it.

Let me know if you ever find yourself here :)

Tales Volume I

The international best seller and social media phenomena that started it all!

"Tales from your dreams and beyond. With over 20 million views across TikTok and Instagram, Tales is loved by readers around the world.

Told from the perspective of a conductor on a train that travels through countless different worlds, Tales is a collection of over 40 short stories. Each story explores a new world, all of them accessible via The Station Between Worlds.

From worlds where you can relive your happiest memories again and again, ice worlds where time slows down and sinister seaside carnival worlds, to a train that takes passengers to their soulmates, a movie theatre where you can watch all of your past lives and a doctor who cures broken hearts, Tales transports readers to places where anything is possible.

Paperback and hardback back editions feature full colour, full page illustrations bringing the Tales to life.

Imagination is a taste of infinity. Let's explore these infinite worlds of imagination together.

David Jones (also known as storydj) is an internationally best selling poet and storyteller followed by over 1 million readers."

Available as a paperback, hardback and Kindle eBook.

And Coming Soon…Tales The Novel.

A full length fantasy novel set across all of the worlds. The novel will be released on October 1st 2023 and it represents the final chapter of the Tales story.

"Perhaps you are wondering how I know about all these worlds? Would you believe me if I told you that I made them up, or is that too implausible? I will give you a more reasonable explanation. Long ago, I was the conductor on a train. It took people across all of the worlds, too many for me to write about and too many even for me to remember. That train was only one of many that passed through the Station Between Worlds, speeding across train tracks like neurones to the far corners of the multiverse. Is that more believable than my making it all up? I think so. It is important for me to be believed because I must tell you a story. It is the story of the worlds, but it is also the story of how there were nearly no worlds at all. The story is vital, so it would be easier if you simply chose to believe it, without me having to convince you. Is that a deal that we could make, you and I? Just for now? Please?"

Interested readers can signup via the bio link on David's social media to be notified the moment the book goes on sale.

More Books By David Jones.

Tales Volume I.
Love And Space Dust.
Love And Space Dust Volume II.
loud world, quiet thoughts.
Love As The Stars Went Out.
Could You Ever Live Without?
Moonlight & You.
Highway Heart.
Death's Door.

Social media.

Instagram: @storydj and @storydj.tales
TikTok: @story.dj
Facebook: thestorydj

SubStack.

SubStack subscribers can signup to receive new stories direct to their inbox every week. The subscription also includes unseen illustrations of the worlds, news about books and more.

Subscribe at https://storydjtales.substack.com

Printed in Great Britain
by Amazon